To my children,
Ella and Jackson,
for inspiring me
to inspire you.
And to my Gram and
Andrew for reminding
me of the beauty of
everlasting love.

The Secret To Beating The Dragon
Lynn Reilly
Tradepaper ISBN: 9781945026324
Library of Congress Control Number: 2017939531

Published by Sacred Stories Publishing, LLC
Delray Beach, FL
www.sacredstoriespublishing.com

Printed in the United States of America

The Secret to
Beating
The
Dragon

Lynn Reilly

Art By Mikaela San Pietro

Andrew and
his Gram,
were the very
best of friends.

She'd sit and listen for hours
to the stories he would bend.

They'd plan their great adventures over a shared cup of tea.

Always conquering imaginary dragons,
and saving the village from tragedy.

Thousands of
adventures they'd planned,
and the ending
always the same.

Always conquering imaginary dragons,
and saving the village from tragedy.

As the hero and heroine in front of the crowd,
Gram would always exclaim,
"We are here today,
But we may not be tomorrow.

No need to fear,
Or wallow in your sorrow.

The secret to beating the dragon,
Is to look him straight in the eye.

And watch as he scurries away,
For bravery he cannot get by."

As Andrew grew older, so did his Gram,

and their stories began to slow down.

They still traveled
to faraway places,
and scared the
dragon out of town.

But Gram grew tired very quickly,
and Andrew knew he must tell the
villagers of the dragon's defeat.
Still Gram would whisper at the end,
to prove the dragon was beat.

Gram's whispers became softer and softer,
until her words disappeared into the air.

Her body no longer walked the Earth, and Andrew fell into despair.

Andrew spent his days feeling alone, missing his Gram and their imaginary travels.

His dreams were filled with dragons, but he was now alone in his battles.

One day Andrew returned to Gram's house,
to pick up a box of toys he left there.

And when he reached
inside he found
something familiar,
the teacup he and Gram used
for the tea they
would share!

He turned the cup over, and saw a note taped to the base.
"To Andrew, Love Gram" written boldly, with a big smiley face.

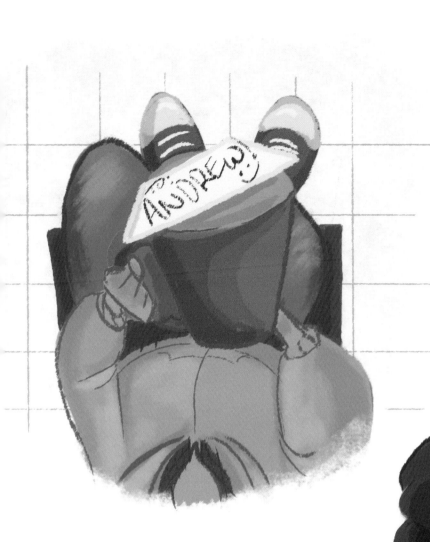

"We are here today,
But we may not
be tomorrow.
No need to fear,
Or wallow in
your sorrow.

The secret to
beating the Dragon,
Is to look him
straight in the eye.
And watch as
he scurries away,
For bravery he
cannot get by."

We are here today,
but we may not be tomorrow.
No need to fear,
or wallow in your sorrow.

The secret to beating the Dragon
is to look him straight in the
And watch as he scurries a
for bravery he cannot get by.

Your strength is your faith,
and even after we walk away,
the spirit of our gifts to you,
are always here to stay.

— Gram ;)

Your strength is in your faith,
and even after we walk away,
the spirit of our gifts to you,
are always here to stay."

It was then that
Andrew knew,
in the bottom of his heart,
that Gram was still
with him, and
had been from
the start.

Andrew still misses
his Gram each day,
his closest and
very best friend.
But he knows their
adventures continue,
and won't ever come
to an end.

CPSIA information can be obtained at www.ICGtesting.com
Printed in the USA
BVIW12n2332230517
484548BV00002B/2